ANN JUNGMAN is the author of over 100 children's titles, including the bestselling *Vlad the Drac*. Ann's books for Frances Lincoln include *The Prince who thought he was a Rooster* and *The Most Magnificent Mosque*. She is also the founder of Barn Owl Books.

RUSSELL AYTO took his Degree in Graphics at Exeter College of Art and Design. He has won and been listed for various prizes for his children's books, including *The Witch's Children*, shortlisted for the Kate Greenaway Medal, and *The Witch's Children and the Queen*, which won the Smarties Gold Award in 2003. *Cinderella and the Hot Air Balloon* was his first book for Frances Lincoln.

For Cressida and Hugh – A.J.
For Lisa and Natalie Mort – R.A.

Cinderella and the Hot Air Balloon copyright © Frances Lincoln Limited 1992
Text copyright © Ann Jungman 1992
Illustrations copyright © Russell Ayto 1992

First published in Great Britain in 1992 by
Frances Lincoln Children's Books, 4 Torriano Mews,
Torriano Avenue, London NW5 2RZ
www.franceslincoln.com

This paperback edition published in Great Britain and the USA in 2007

British Library Cataloguing in Publication Data available on request

ISBN 978-1-84507-710-5

Illustrated with pen and ink and watercolour

Set in Bembo

Printed in China

1 3 5 7 9 8 6 4 2

Cinderella
and the
Hot Air Balloon

Ann Jungman • Russell Ayto

F

FRANCES LINCOLN
CHILDREN'S BOOKS

Long ago and far away there lived a rich merchant
with three daughters.

The two eldest, Ermentrude and Esmerelda, liked
to comb their hair, try on clothes, polish their nails,
and gossip.

Ella, the youngest, was different. She liked to
climb trees, ride horses bareback, skate on thin ice,
and run barefoot.

What Ella liked most of all was to talk to Cook and the other servants round the kitchen fire. Often they cooked potatoes in the cinders and ate them with melted butter dripping down their fingers.

"Fancy talking to the servants when you could be up here with us," sneered Esmerelda.

"You spend so much time among the cinders, we ought to call you Cinderella," jeered Ermentrude.

Ella laughed. "I wouldn't mind. I'd like it better than boring old Ella." So from that day on, Ella was known as Cinderella.

One day a messenger came with invitations to a ball at the palace.

"How wonderful!" cried Esmerelda. "I shall go in green silk and dripping with diamonds."

"I shall wear my purple satin," declared Ermentrude, "and dear Mother's emeralds."

"Boring!" muttered Cinderella. "And I *shan't* go."

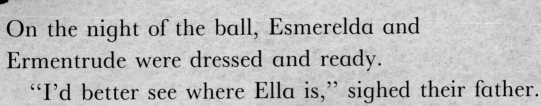

On the night of the ball, Esmerelda and
Ermentrude were dressed and ready.

"I'd better see where Ella is," sighed their father.

He found her huddled in bed. "I'm feeling ill,
father," she cried. "You'll have to go without me.
Have a wonderful time."

As the coach drove away, Cinderella leapt out of bed and raced down to the kitchen.

"I didn't want to go to the boring old ball," she explained. "I'd much rather eat potatoes here with you."

At that moment, Cinderella's Fairy Godmother appeared.

"Fear not, Cinderella!" she cried. "You *shall* go to the ball!"

"Oh no, Fairy Godmother," Cinderella begged. "I really don't want to go to the ball."

"You mean you don't want a beautiful ball dress and glass slippers?"

"No," insisted Cinderella. "I've got masses of dresses, but the maids and Cook haven't. Please make ball gowns for them instead."

So the Fairy Godmother did just that.

What's more, at Cinderella's suggestion she turned a pumpkin into a coach and mice into footmen so that the servants could have a real night out.

Soon the maids and Cook were bundled into the coach, and off they went all around the town.

They had so much fun that the next time the coach passed the house, the Fairy Godmother clambered in beside them.

Cinderella stayed in the kitchen to bake potatoes and rustle up some pumpkin soup.

When the travellers got back, they tucked in.

"What now?" asked Cook.

"Let's have our own dance," suggested Cinderella. "Godmother, could you turn some frogs into musicians so we can have our own band?"

"All right," said the Fairy Godmother. "And I'll turn some frogs into young men, so you all have partners to dance with."

The frog band had two trumpets, a double bass,
a set of drums, and the grandest piano you ever saw.

Soon everyone was having the time of their lives.

The neighbours heard the music and came to join
in. Before long there were so many people that the
dance spilled out into the garden and the noise
could be heard at the palace.

The King's guests began to leave the ball to go to Cinderella's party. After a while, even the King and Queen came to join in the fun.

Cinderella climbed a tree and watched the party with great satisfaction.

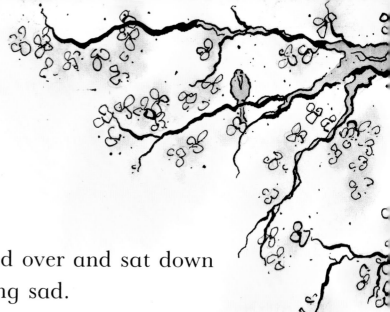

A young man wandered over and sat down beneath the tree, looking sad.

Cinderella swung down to land beside him.

"Hello, I'm Cinderella. This is my party, well, sort of."

"I'm Prince Charming," the young man said with a sigh. "Isn't that the worst name you ever heard?"

"Choose another one then," said Cinderella. "I think people should do what they like."

"I've always dreamed of being called Bill," he told her.

"That's a good name," agreed Cinderella. "Come on, Bill. Let's go and join in the dancing."

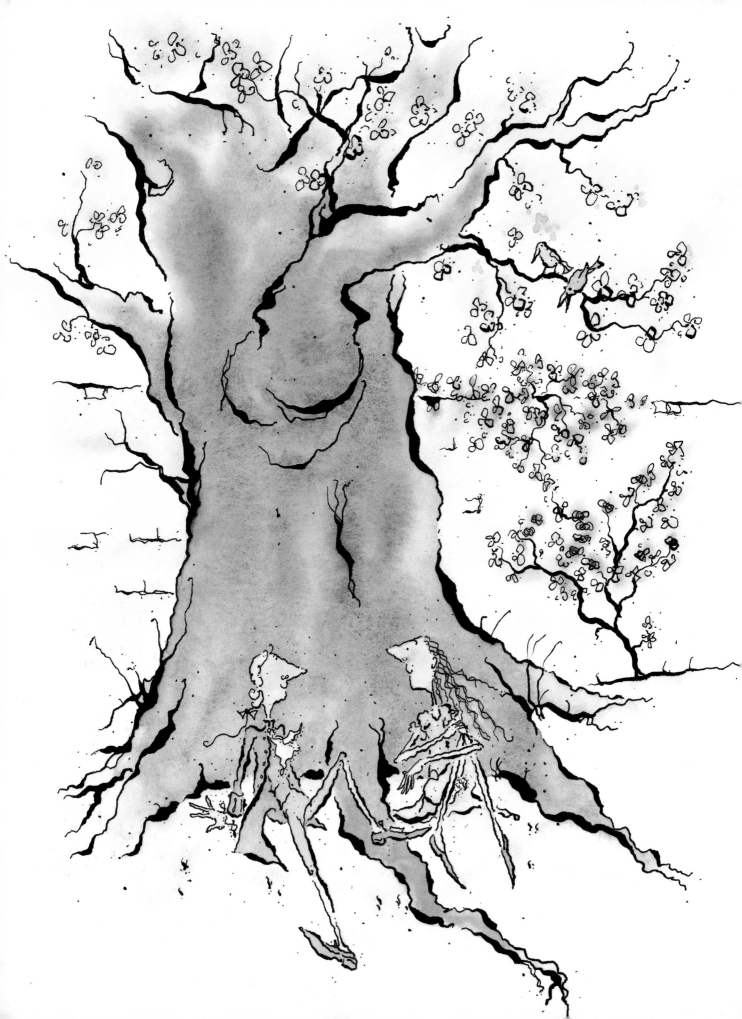

"I'll dance if you want to," Bill said, "but to be honest, I don't really like dancing. What I really like is climbing trees, riding bareback, skating on thin ice and running barefoot."

"So do I!" cried Cinderella. "Let's run away together and do the things we like all day long."

"My father wouldn't let me. When he catches up with me I'll be in terrible trouble. Oh no!"

As he spoke Bill caught sight of the King. At the same instant, Cinderella spotted her father and sisters.

"Don't despair, Bill!" Cinderella cried. "Go and find a big pumpkin while I fetch my Fairy Godmother."

She dragged her Fairy Godmother away from the dancing. "Now, Fairy Godmother, I *really* need your help. Please, please turn the pumpkin into a hot air balloon as fast as you can."

The Fairy Godmother waved her wand. There in the middle of the lawn stood a wonderful, multi-coloured hot air balloon.

"Get in quick, Bill," yelled Cinderella as the balloon rose into the air.

"Come back this instant," shouted Cinderella's father and sisters.

"Charming, come down this minute," bellowed the King, "or I'll never forgive you."

"Goodbye Cinderella," called the crowd.

Bill and Cinderella waved. "We'll write to you," they shouted. "Byeee!"

And the balloon floated out of sight.

3

MORE TITLES FROM
FRANCES LINCOLN CHILDREN'S BOOKS

The Most Magnificent Mosque

Ann Jungman

Illustrated by Shelley Fowles

When a new Christian King decides to pull down the
beautiful Mosque of Cordoba, three old friends decide
something must be done on behalf of all the citizens,
whether Muslim, Jew or Christian…

ISBN 978-1-84507-085-4

Climbing Rosa

Shelley Fowles

Rosa can climb anything from a tree to a drainpipe –
which is just as well since her nasty stepmother and stepsister
make her sleep on the roof. So when the king offers his son's
hand in marriage to the girl who can bring down some seeds
from the enormous tree growing in the palace grounds,
Rosa decides to have a go…

ISBN 978-1-84507-079-3

Sausages

Jessica Souhami

When an elf rewards John's kindness with three wishes,
John and his wife start thinking of all the lovely things
they could have. But it is so difficult to choose and,
as the hours pass, John starts to feel hungry…

ISBN 978-1-84507-397-8

Frances Lincoln titles are available from all good bookshops.
You can also buy books and find out more about your favourite titles,
authors and illustrators on our website: www.franceslincoln.com